Brady Brady
and the Most Important Game

Written by Mary Shaw

Illustrated by Chuck Temple

Scholastic Canada Ltd.

Toronto   New York   London   Auckland   Sydney
Mexico City   New Delhi   Hong Kong   Buenos Aires

Scholastic Canada Ltd.
604 King Street West, Toronto, Ontario M5V 1E1, Canada

Scholastic Inc.
557 Broadway, New York, NY 10012, USA

Scholastic Australia Pty Limited
PO Box 579, Gosford, NSW 2250, Australia

Scholastic New Zealand Limited
Private Bag 94407, Botany, Manukau 2163, New Zealand

Scholastic Children's Books
Euston House, 24 Eversholt Street, London NW1 1DB, UK

www.scholastic.ca

Library and Archives Canada Cataloguing in Publication

Title: Brady Brady and the most important game / written by Mary Shaw ; illustrated by Chuck Temple.
Names: Shaw, Mary, 1965- author. | Temple, Chuck, 1962- illustrator.
Identifiers: Canadiana 20190125357 | ISBN 9781443175333 (soft cover)
Subjects: LCSH: Brady Brady (Fictitious character)—Juvenile fiction. | LCSH: Sportsmanship—Juvenile fiction. | CSH: Hockey stories, Canadian (English)
Classification: LCC PS8587.H3473 B735 2019 | DDC jC813/.6—dc23

Originally published in 2004 by Brady Brady Inc.
This edition published in 2020 by Scholastic Canada Ltd.

6 5 4 3 2 1   Printed in Malaysia 108   20 21 22 23 24

Brady had been taking shots on Chester all morning. When Chester needed a break, Hatrick took his spot in net. Brady and his friend were determined to practice. This weekend they would play in the biggest hockey tournament of the season, **_The Gold Stick_**.

Not only was it the biggest tournament of the season, it was being played at the Icehogs' home rink. The Icehog players put up posters all over town to let everyone know about the important weekend.

Brady had been counting the days until the big weekend arrived. The night before the tournament, Brady was so excited, he slept in his equipment.

He dreamt about racing up the ice on a breakaway, sparks flying from his skates, and scoring the tournament-winning goal.

When Brady yelled "***he scores!!!***" in his sleep, Hatrick jumped right out of his basket.

Brady high-fived his teammates as they arrived in the dressing room. All the Icehogs agreed that tournaments were the best part of playing hockey. Everyone was excited about meeting other players and trading team pins at center ice.

The stands were packed with parents, grandparents, brothers, sisters, and players from other teams.

When Tree sang the anthem at the opening game,
the crowd went wild!

The Icehogs battled hard every game and their efforts paid off. The next day, they would be playing for *The Gold Stick*.

"Make sure you eat a healthy dinner and get a good night's sleep," their coach told them.

"Oh, and Brady Brady, don't forget to dry out your smelly hockey gloves," he said with a wink.

Brady slept in his equipment again that night.

On the morning of their most important game, the Icehogs arrived early to find out who they would be playing against. A loud groan could be heard throughout the rink as the coach announced . . . "Team, we're playing the **Dragoons**!"

The Dragoons loved to wait until the referee had his back turned, and then see how many Icehogs they could trip.

Tes bit her bottom lip. Tree hummed nervously. Brady tied Chester's skates together so that he couldn't run away.

When everyone was dressed, they gathered in the center of the room for their team cheer.

"We've got the power,
We've got the might,
Hey Dragoons,
Kiss the Gold Stick good night!"

Out on the rink, the Icehogs lined up against the Dragoons.

The ref dropped the puck and the game began. The Dragoons tripped and slashed, and played a pretty mean game, but the Icehogs did not give up.

The Dragoons' coach played his best player most of the game. Some Dragoons did not get to play at all.

The Icehogs' coach told his players, "We made it here as a team, and everyone on the team will play."

The game was tied as the third period began, and the Icehogs were bruised and battered.

The Dragoons had been spraying snow in Chester's mask all game.

Tes had been bodychecked while doing her Twirlin' Torpedo.

Gregory was slashed on a breakaway.

Never in his life had Brady wanted to win a game so badly.

There was only a minute left to go in the game, and then it happened.

The Dragoons' best player got a breakaway — the same breakaway that Brady had dreamt about.

Chester could barely see through the snow spray on his glasses.

The Dragoon fired the puck top shelf, past Chester's outstretched glove hand and into the Icehogs' net. The Dragoon raised his arms in victory.

Brady could see the Dragoons' fans in the stands whistling and screaming at the top of their lungs. The Icehogs' fans were leaving the stands. Brady's dad gave him a weak smile as he walked past the glass.

The final seconds of the game seemed to last forever. Finally, the buzzer sounded. The game was over. The Icehogs had lost ***The Gold Stick***.

Reluctantly, the team lined up to shake hands with the Dragoons, and then skated off the ice with their heads lowered.

The dressing room was silent. Tears rolled down several of the Icehogs' faces. Chester buried his head between his pads.

Brady didn't like to lose. Losing made his heart feel heavy.

Coach walked to the center of the room with a **huge** smile on his face. "Icehogs, I know it's hard right now, but try to remember how hard you worked to get to this final game. And if you learn only one thing in your hockey lives, remember this: it's more important to lose fairly than to win by cheating."

The Icehogs began to take off their equipment. Suddenly, there was a loud knock on the dressing room door. Brady peeked his head out.

"**Wait!** Everyone keep your equipment on!" Brady yelled to his friends. "That wasn't our most important game. The **next** one is!"

When Brady flung open the door, the Icehogs collapsed with laughter when they saw who would meet them on the ice.

Brady didn't know who was more excited
about the most important game —
the Icehogs or their parents.
But he did know that his heart
didn't feel heavy anymore.